This
Bear with Sticky Paws
book belongs to:

· · · · · · · · · · · · · · · · ·

KEEP YOUR PAWS OFF!

*for Jack,
with love*

ORCHARD BOOKS
338 Euston Road, London NW1 3BH
Orchard Books Australia
Level 17/207 Kent Street, Sydney, NSW 2000

First published in 2009
by Orchard Books
Text and illustrations © Clara Vulliamy 2009
The right of Clara Vulliamy to be identified as
the author and illustrator of this work has been
asserted by her in accordance with the
Copyright, Designs and Patents Act, 1988.

A CIP catalogue record for this book
is available from the British Library.

ISBN 978 1 40830 064 0
1 3 5 7 9 10 8 6 4 2
Printed in China
Orchard Books is a division of Hachette Children's Books,
an Hachette UK Company.
www.hachette.co.uk

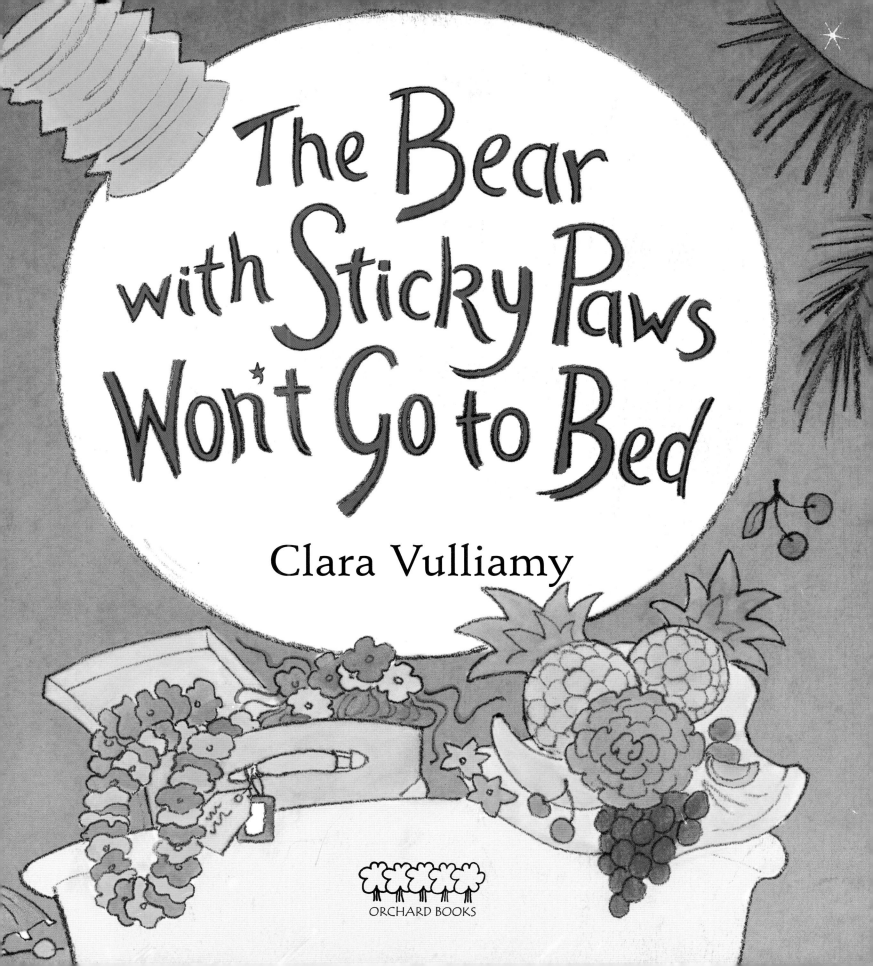

The Bear with Sticky Paws Won't Go to Bed

Clara Vulliamy

ORCHARD BOOKS

There's a girl called Pearl and she's very wide awake. She says,

"I'm really really really **busy** and I'm **not** going to **sleep!**"

"I'll put this all away,"
says Mum,
"ready for tomorrow,
and tuck you up."

"I won't lie down.

I won't shut my eyes.

I don't want to play tomorrow –

I want to play NOW!"

And she jumps out of bed!

But then,

bing-
bong!

There's a bear on the doorstep,
a small white tufty one,
standing on his suitcase to reach the bell.

"Bedtime?" says the bear.
"Not Bedtime!
PARTY TIME!"

Now he's bouncing on the bed,
standing on his head . . .
"Let's do an ADVENTURE!" says the bear.
"OK," says Pearl. "I'm not sleepy!"

"ALL ABOARD!"
says the bear.

"Hold on tight . . ."

"HIGHER!" says the bear,
flying up and up, over treetops
and chimneypots . . .

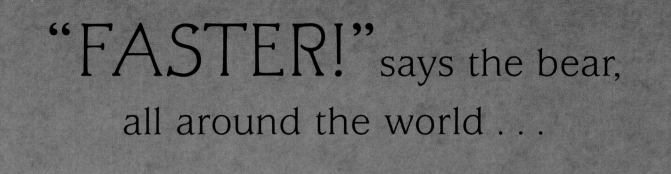

"FASTER!" says the bear,
all around the world . . .

"SPLASH!"

"The party's HERE!" says the bear.
"Oh good – I love parties," says Pearl.

The bear has

10 colourful cocktails

9 ice cream sundaes

and 8 sugar fancies.

And – oh NO!
Sticky paws everywhere!

"Let's do SAND!" says the bear.
"OK," says Pearl. "I'm not sleepy!"
Pearl makes

7 perfect sand castles

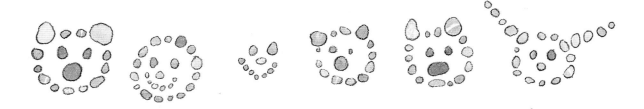

6 pebble faces

and 5 patterns of pretty shells.

The bear is practising his BIG jumps,
and – oh NO!
Everything gets knocked over.

"Let's play VOLLEYBALL! I WIN!"
says the bear,
running off with the ball.

"Not sleepy . . ." says Pearl.

"I NEVER sleep!" says the bear.

"COCONUTS!"

"Maybe tomorrow . . ." says Pearl.
"NOW!" says the bear.

"PARTY CLOTHES!"
The bear wears

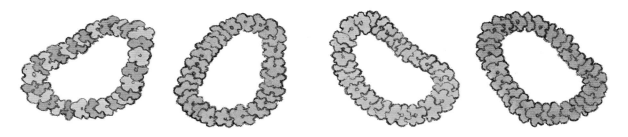

4 flower garlands

3 hula skirts

and 2 huge hats.

"FRUITY!"
says the bear.

"A little bit sleepy," says Pearl.
"NOT SLEEPY!" says the bear.

"TIME FOR DANCING!"

Whirling and twirling,

wilder and wilder . . .

until Pearl calls out . . .

"NO MORE! It's my bedtime."

"Not MY bedtime!" says the bear.

"GOODBYE!"

The bear is dancing,
dancing away,

and Pearl's eyes are
closing, closing.

"Sleepy," says Pearl.
"Sleep tight," says Mum.

And there's still time . . .

. . . for 1 last goodnight kiss.